STONE ARCH BOOKS
a capstone imprint

Sports Illustrated KIDS

You Can't Spike Your Serves

by Julie Gassman

illustrated by Jorge Santillan

STONE ARCH BOOKS
a capstone imprint

VICTORY SCHOOL SUPERSTARS

Sports Illustrated KIDS *You Can't Spike Your Serves*
is published by Stone Arch Books — A Capstone Imprint
151 Good Counsel Drive, P.O. Box 669
Mankato, Minnesota 56002
www.capstonepub.com

Art Director and Designer: Bob Lentz
Creative Director: Heather Kindseth
Production Specialist: Michelle Biedscheid

Timeline photo credits: Shutterstock/Fornax (top right),
olly (top left), Robyn Mackenzie (middle right); Sports
Illustrated/Al Tielemans (bottom), Bob Rosato (middle
left).

Library of Congress Cataloging-in-Publication Data is
available on the Library of Congress website.

ISBN: 978-1-4342-2231-2 (library binding)
ISBN: 978-1-4342-3080-5 (paperback)

Summary: Alicia plans a volleyball tournament.

Printed in the United States of America in Stevens Point, Wisconsin.
092010   005934WZS11

TABLE of CONTENTS

ALICIA GOHL

Volleyball

AGE: 10
GRADE: 4
SUPER SPORTS ABILITY: Super Jumping

CARMEN   ALICIA   JOSH   DANNY   KENZIE   TYLER

VICTORY SCHOOL MAP

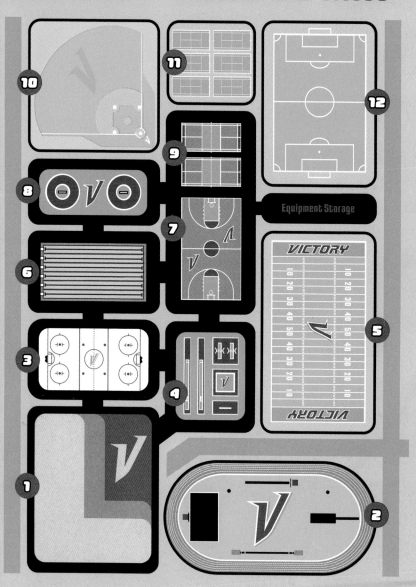

1. Main Offices/Classrooms
2. Track and Field
3. Hockey/Figure Skating
4. Gymnastics
5. Football
6. Swimming
7. Basketball
8. Wrestling
9. Volleyball
10. Baseball/Softball
11. Tennis
12. Soccer

Equipment Storage

Surprise Assembly

"Hey, Alicia, wait up!"

I hear my friend Carmen's voice behind me as I walk toward the school theater. "Hi, Carmen," I say. "Great game last night!" Carmen is a star on the girls' basketball team. She never loses that ball!

"Thanks!" she says with a grin. "I'm so excited we have an assembly! Isn't that great? I love assemblies!"

I laugh at her excitement. "Do you know what it's about?" I ask. "I didn't hear anything."

"No, it's a surprise. But I think we are having a guest speaker," she says.

"Oh, good," I say, "I've been so distracted this week. I was worried that I just missed the announcement!"

"Why are you distracted? Do you have a big cheer competition coming up?" she asks.

I am a cheerleader here at the Victory School for Super Athletes. Like all the students at Victory, I have a super skill — jumping. I jump so high and far that during one of our routines, I leap up to the middle of the bleachers. In one jump!

"No, that's not it," I say. "I got a letter from my pen pal, Jenny. We met at cheer camp this summer. Her cheerleading team has a problem, and I want to help."

"What's the problem?" Carmen asks.

I tell her that Jenny's team's pom-poms are falling apart. They are really old. But their school doesn't have any money to buy new ones.

"How much money could pom-poms cost? They're just plastic," says Carmen.

"More than you'd think — about five hundred dollars!" I say.

"Wow, that's a lot! But I don't see how you can help with their problem," says Carmen as we reach the theater and find our seats.

"I thought I could hold a fund-raiser and give them all the money we raise. But I'm not sure what to do," I say.

"How about a bake sale?" Carmen suggests.

"There have been three bake sales this month alone. People are sick of brownies," I say.

"Sick of brownies? Impossible!" she says, laughing. "But I get what you are saying. Don't worry, Alicia. You'll think of something. You always have great ideas."

CHAPTER 2

Introducing Reece Robinson

"Good morning, Victory," says Principal Armstrong. "I'm happy to start the day with a surprise assembly."

We all cheer. Assemblies at Victory are always exciting. At the last one, we cheered on sumo wrestlers from Japan.

"We have a special guest this morning," he continues. "She will be working with us for a few weeks to teach a special session on volleyball. Let's welcome Reece Robinson."

We start cheering as soon as Principal Armstrong says her name. Everyone knows who Reece Robinson is! We all watched her lead her team to gold in the Olympics last summer.

The volleyball star takes the microphone. "Hi, everybody!" she says. "Let me start by saying that I would like everyone here to call me Reece."

She continues, "I am very excited to spend some time here at Victory. You will all see me in your regular gym class starting next week."

Everyone starts cheering again. Who better to learn volleyball from than the one and only Reece Robinson?

"I'm glad you are all so excited," Reece says with a grin.

She continues, "We are going to cover the basics of volleyball. I hope you will like the sport as much as I do. And I can't wait to see all of your super skills. Does anyone have any questions?"

A boy in the front raises his hand and says, "The last time we had a special teacher was in basketball. Before he left, we had a three-on-three tournament to really practice our skills. Will we do something like that?"

"Hmm . . . let me think about that, and I will get back to you in gym class," says Reece.

She glances at her watch, then adds, "If anyone else has questions, I will be in my office after school today. Room 204. Now it is time to get to class."

I turn to Carmen. "That's it!" I say.

"What's it?" she asks.

"A volleyball tournament! It's the perfect fund-raiser," I say.

CHAPTER 3

My Idea

I've been waiting to talk to Reece about my idea all day. Finally, school is over, and I get my chance. When I get to Reece's office, I knock on her open door. "Excuse me, Reece?" I say.

"Yes," she says. "Come on in." She gives me a warm smile as I take a seat.

"My name is Alicia. I'm in fourth grade," I say.

"Nice to meet you," says Reece. "What can I do for you?"

I share my idea with her. I tell her that I would like to organize a volleyball tournament to raise money for Jenny's squad.

"Teams can pay a fee to play. We can sell food, too," I explain.

"That is a great idea! I'll take care of getting the okay from Principal Armstrong and organizing everything with the school," says Reece.

"And I will take care of letting everyone know! I make great posters," I say. "Do you think it would be okay to invite Jenny's cheer team to compete?"

"Of course! The more teams we have, the stronger the tournament," says Reece.

"Thanks, Reece! I'm so excited," I say. We agree to meet again in a few days to talk about what we've done. I can't wait to get started!

CHAPTER 4

The First Class

Today is my first gym class with Reece. She calls us all together. "Hello, fourth graders," she says. "Today we will do some drills to learn the positions in volleyball. Let's start with setting."

Reece shows us how to toss the ball up so we can set. As the ball comes down, she holds her arms above her head. Then she uses her fingertips to send the ball back up.

"Now it is in position for another player to spike the ball over the net," she explains.

We all practice setting the ball. Everyone is laughing and having a great time. It takes me some time, but I finally catch on to setting.

"Okay, now let's try spiking," says Reece. "Carmen, could you come and set the ball for me? Then I will spike it over the net."

Carmen sets the ball, and *SMACK*, Reece hammers it over the net! When I realize how important jumping is to spiking, I feel confident. After all, I'm Victory's best jumper.

"Now partner up and take turns setting and spiking," says Reece.

I partner with Carmen, who is great at setting.

"You can spike first," she says. As the ball comes down toward me, I leap.

Because I can get so high with my jumps, I am able to hit the ball with a lot of force. Sometimes, though, I jump right over it, which makes us giggle.

"This is fun!" I say, as Carmen and I switch positions. After a little longer, Reece tells us that it is time to try serving.

Reece shows us two ways to serve, underhand and overhand. "Try both ways," she tells us.

First I try an underhand serve. I balance the ball in front of me in my left hand. Then I swing my right arm forward to hit the ball.

Instead of sailing over the net, though, it falls to the ground. I try a few more times, but I keep coming up short.

Maybe I will try overhand instead, I think.

I throw the ball up like Reece had shown us. Without thinking, I jump up. Slightly above the ball, I hit it with my right hand, but it slams toward the ground.

Reece must have seen the whole thing. "Nice try, Alicia, but you can't spike your serves," she teases. "Try again, and keep those feet on the floor."

I try again, but my feet keep leaping up. After a dozen more tries, I still haven't gotten one serve over the net. I better figure this serving thing out before the tournament, or I don't think I'll want to play.

The Jump Serve

It's our last gym class before the volleyball tournament tomorrow. That means it is the last day I have to fix my serves. I still can't get my serves to go over the net.

"Hello, everybody," says Reece. "Today, I would like to split you up. Half of you can play a game of volleyball, while I help the rest of you on your drills. Then we will switch."

She reads the names of kids she wants to work with first and then sends the others over to start their game. Of course, I am on her list of kids who need help.

"Okay, let's start with serving," she says. "Alicia, I want to work with you first."

I walk over slowly. I have had such a tough time with serving that I really dread practicing it.

"Alicia, I have an idea to help you with your serving," says Reece.

"You do?" I ask.

"Yes, and I'm sorry I didn't think of it sooner. It's just that this type of serve is a little more advanced," says Reece.

"I am NOT ready for anything advanced when it comes to serving," I insist.

"Trust me. This type of serve is going to play to your talents. You will just need to get the timing right," she says.

Reece explains that I will be doing a jump serve. "You will take a few steps toward the ball and jump up as you hit it. Be sure to stay behind the ball, not above it," she says.

She shows me how to do it. I see how my jumping will help me with this serve. I'll just have to get the steps right. I give it a try. The ball falls short, but the serve feels good.

"Try it again," says Reece. So I do, and this time it goes over!

"Yes, I did it!" I say.

"Thataway! Keep practicing. I want you to nail your serves at tomorrow's tournament," says Reece.

Tournament Day

CHAPTER 6

I take a final look around the gym.
Everything is ready for the tournament.
I spot some familiar red curls across the
room. It's Jenny! I start leaping toward her.
"Hi, Jenny!" I yell.

"Alicia, hi! I am so excited for today. Thanks again for everything you did for us," she says.

"I'm just so glad we could help. Come with me. I have a special announcement to make before the tournament starts," I say.

We make our way to the front of the gym, where the microphone is.

Jenny laughs. "I have to admit something," she says. "For a while this week, I didn't want to come and play today. I was afraid I would be terrible, and it wouldn't be any fun."

"I know what you mean. I was worried, too, especially about my serves," I say. "But I figured them out."

"Oh, well, I will probably still be terrible. But I'm not going to let it ruin my fun," says Jenny. "I mean, how can I be upset when someone did all this for my squad? The least I can do is enjoy it."

"I never thought of it like that," I say. "But you are right! The fund-raiser is the most important thing today. That reminds me . . ."

I take the microphone. "Hello, everybody. Welcome and thank you for taking part today. Before the first games get underway, I have an announcement."

I continue. "Jenny Sprang is here from Red Sky School in Morristown. Her cheerleading team needs new pom-poms, and we are here to help!"

I pause as everyone cheers. "Jenny,"
I say, "With the team entry fees for today,
we raised $500. Here is a check to cover the
cost of your pom-poms."

I hand the microphone back to the
announcer and turn to Jenny. She grabs me
into a hug before I have a chance to say
anything.

"Thank you so much!" she says. "This is amazing!"

"I'm so happy I could help!" I say. "Now let's get going. I have some serves to nail!"

GLOSSARY

announcement (uh-NOUNS-ment)—a public notice that says something important

assembly (uh-SEM-blee)—a meeting of lots of people, often for entertainment

competition (kom-puh-TISH-uhn)—a contest

distracted (diss-TRAKT-ed)—to be unable to focus on what you are doing

dread (DRED)—to be very unwilling to do something

fund-raiser (FUHND-RAYZ-er)—an event held to raise money for a special reason

routines (roo-TEENS)—performances that are carefully worked out so they can be repeated often

serving (SURV-ing)—hitting a ball over a net to begin play in volleyball

tournament (TUR-nuh-muhnt)—a series of contests in which many teams try to win a championship

JULIE GASSMAN

The youngest in a family of nine children, Julie Gassman grew up in Howard, South Dakota. After college, she traded in small-town life for the world of magazine publishing in New York City. She now lives in southern Minnesota with her husband and their three children. She is also the author of *Cheerleading Really Is a Sport* and *Nobody Wants to Play with a Ball Hog* from the Victory School Superstars series.

ABOUT THE ILLUSTRATOR

JORGE SANTILLAN

Jorge Santillan got his start illustrating in the children's sections of local newspapers. He opened his own illustration studio in 2005. His creative team specializes in books, comics, and children magazines. Jorge lives in Mendoza, Argentina, with his wife, Bety; son, Luca; and their four dogs, Fito, Caro, Angie, and Sammy.

VOLLEYBALL IN HISTORY

1895 Volleyball is invented by William G. Morgan in Holyoke, Massachusetts.

1900 A **special ball** is made and official rules are published for the sport.

1917 Volleyball is introduced in Europe and Africa by American soldiers fighting in World War I.

1924 Volleyball is demonstrated at the **Paris Olympic Games.**

1964 Volleyball is played as an Olympic medal sport for the first time at the Tokyo games.

1984 The United States wins its first Olympic gold medal in volleyball in Los Angeles, California.

1987 The first Beach Volleyball World Championship is played in Brazil.

1995 Volleyball turns **100 years old**.

1996 Beach volleyball becomes an Olympic sport at the Atlanta games.

2007 **Misty May-Treanor** becomes the women's all-time wins leader in beach volleyball.

2008 The **U.S. men's team** takes gold at the Bejing Olympics.

VICTORY SCHOOL SUPERSTARS

Five Fouls and You're Out!

It's a Wrestling Mat, Not a Dance Floor

There's a Hurricane In the Pool!

There's No Crying in Baseball

Who Wants to Play Just for Kicks?

You Can't Spike Your Serves

Read them ALL!

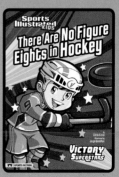

THE FUN DOESN'T STOP HERE!

Discover more at . . .

www.CAPSTONEKIDS.com

- Videos & Contests
- Games & Puzzles
- Heroes & Villains
- Authors & Illustrators

STONE ARCH BOOKS
a capstone imprint